Schoolhouse in the Woods

OTHER YEARLING BOOKS YOU WILL ENJOY:

THE HAPPY LITTLE FAMILY, *Rebecca Caudill*
UP AND DOWN THE RIVER, *Rebecca Caudill*
SCHOOLROOM IN THE PARLOR, *Rebecca Caudill*
SATURDAY COUSINS, *Rebecca Caudill*
ALL-OF-A-KIND FAMILY, *Sydney Taylor*
ALL-OF-A-KIND FAMILY DOWNTOWN, *Sydney Taylor*
ALL-OF-A-KIND FAMILY UPTOWN, *Sydney Taylor*
MORE ALL-OF-A-KIND FAMILY, *Sydney Taylor*
ELLA OF ALL-OF-A-KIND FAMILY, *Sydney Taylor*
THE VELVET ROOM, *Zilpha Keatley Snyder*

YEARLING BOOKS/YOUNG YEARLINGS/YEARLING CLASSICS are designed especially to entertain and enlighten young people. Patricia Reilly Giff, consultant to this series, received the bachelor's degree from Marymount College. She holds the master's degree in history from St. John's University, and a Professional Diploma in Reading from Hofstra University. She was a teacher and reading consultant for many years, and is the author of numerous books for young readers.

For a complete listing of all Yearling titles, write to Dell Readers Service, P.O. Box 1045, South Holland, IL 60473.

SCHOOLHOUSE
IN THE
WOODS

By

REBECCA CAUDILL

Pictures by Decie Merwin

A Yearling Book

Published by
Dell Publishing
a division of
Bantam Doubleday Dell Publishing Group, Inc.
666 Fifth Avenue
New York, New York 10103

The author is indebted to *Jack and Jill*, published by The Curtis Publishing Company, and to *Trails*, a magazine for boys and girls published by the Methodist Publishing House, for permission to include in this book the stories that have appeared in those magazines.

ISBN: 0-440-40170-4

Reprinted by arrangement with Henry Holt and Company, Inc.

Printed in the United States of America

June 1989

10 9 8 7 6 5 4 3 2 1

CW

For Clara

*Who walked just ahead of
me down the road to school*

Contents

	PAGE
Waiting for Monday	1
Whose Tree Is This?	18
Grandpap	38
A Day of Surprises	53
The Wind and the Leaves	70
Rain on the Windowpane	87
The Christmas Angel	105

Waiting for Monday

IT WAS Saturday morning, the last day of July. It seemed like an everyday sort of day. Whiskers the cat stretched lazily in the shade of the rose of Sharon bushes. Rover the dog barked at squirrels. The hens cackled, bees buzzed in the blossoms, and heat waves shimmered and danced as they had done every day for a month. But Bonnie knew from the feeling inside her that this was a special day.

Everybody was busy. Mother was making Emmy a dress. She treadled so fast that the little wheel on the sewing machine looked like a silver saucer as it whirled.

Althy was in the back yard washing her long brown hair. Chris was in the woodlot making a bat out of a hickory stick. He whistled as he whittled. Emmy was hunting a hen's nest in the stable loft. Debby was spreading her doll clothes on the rosebush to dry.

Bonnie didn't look busy. She was sitting on the front doorstep, not moving a toe. But she was as busy as busy could be. She was watching for Father. And she was waiting for Monday.

Debby caught sight of Bonnie.

"Are you looking for Father already, Bonnie?" she asked. "Why don't you wash your doll clothes, like me? Then they'll be clean before you start to school Monday. The clock just struck eleven. Father may not be home till sundown."

"I washed my doll clothes yesterday while you were playing at Janie Sawyer's house," said Bonnie. "And ironed them too." And she sat on the doorstep, watching and waiting.

Althy came around the house rubbing her wet hair with a towel. She caught sight of Bonnie sitting on the doorstep.

"You're not watching for Father already, are you, Bonnie?" she asked. "How would you like me to wash your hair? Then it will be clean when you start to school Monday. Father may not be home till supper time."

"Emmy washed my hair yesterday while you were at Aunt Cassie's," said Bonnie. "And curled it too." And she sat on the doorstep, watching and waiting.

Chris came into the kitchen for water to wet the grindstone while he whetted his knife. He caught sight of Bonnie sitting quietly on the doorstep. He stopped whistling.

"Why, Bonnie!" he called. "You're not watching for Father already, are you? Father may not be home till dark. Why don't you get ready to start to school Monday?"

"I got ready yesterday," said Bonnie. And she sat on the doorstep, watching and waiting.

Emmy came from the stable, carrying seven eggs in her apron. She caught sight of Bonnie sitting on the doorstep.

"If you're watching for Father, Bonnie," she said, "he may not be home till you're sound asleep tonight. I'm going to try on my new dress. Want to come?"

Bonnie looked down the road once more. Seeing nobody, she got up from the doorstep and followed Emmy into the house.

Mother looked up from her sewing and smiled. "You're not watching for Father already, are you, Bonnie?" she asked. She finished stitching a seam. "July days are long days, and Father may not be home till midnight. Why don't you run and play?"

Bonnie didn't feel like playing. She didn't wait to see Emmy try on her new dress, either. Instead, she went upstairs quietly, on her tiptoes.

Upstairs, on a long rod, hung all the new clothes Mother had been making for school. There were two new dresses for Althy, size thirteen; two new shirts for Chris, size eleven; one new dress for Emmy, size nine; and two new dresses for Debby, size seven.

At the end of the rod hung two new dresses for Bonnie, size five. One was dark blue, sprinkled with white stars. The other was pink. It had a little ruffle around the neck, a middle-sized ruffle around the sleeves, and a big ruffle at the bottom of the skirt.

On the waist of the pink dress Mother had embroidered a B. Little white flowers were twined about it. It stood for Bonnie. The B was special, because Bonnie was going to wear the dress to school the first day.

Bonnie slipped off her faded, everyday dress, took the pink dress from the rod, and put it on. By trying very hard, she could button all the buttons in the back.

Then she went to look at the schoolbooks which lay on a bench, beside the wall, waiting for Monday.

On the far end of the bench lay two books belonging to Althy. One was a songbook. Althy didn't need the songbook because she knew all the songs by heart. But she liked to carry the book to school anyway.

The other book was a Christmas play. Althy had found it the day before when she was rummaging around in Aunt Cassie's attic. She hoped the teacher, Miss Cora, would let the boys and girls give the play for Christmas, on the last day of school. When Father came home, Althy would have many books, all new, and big and hard to read.

Chris had a tall stack of books. He had a geography, and a history, an arithmetic and a reader, and a spelling book. They had once belonged to Althy. On the flyleaf of each book she had written, "This book belongs to Althy." Chris had erased that. Now the flyleaf read, "This book belongs to Chris."

Emmy's books had belonged to Althy when they were new. Then they had belonged to Chris. Emmy had erased both their names, and had written on the flyleaf of each book, "This book belongs to Emmy."

Debby had four books. They had first belonged to Althy, then to Chris, then to Emmy. The corners were ragged from having been thumbed so often, and the flyleaves had been erased so many times that Debby herself could hardly read what she had written: "This book belongs to Debby." But the words and the pictures inside the books were almost as good as if Father had brought them home yesterday.

At the end of the bench lay an empty blue knapsack. It was Bonnie's, and it was new. Mother had made it for her.

In the knapsack there was a big space for a first reader and a slate. Stitched in one end was a little space for a slate pencil so that it wouldn't break. The knapsack had a long shoulder strap. It was waterproof, so that if Bonnie some morning should get caught in a shower, her first reader wouldn't get wet. And it had a plain big B stitched in red in the corner.

Bonnie lifted the knapsack from the bench, slipped the long strap over her shoulder, and went to the window to see if by any chance Father was coming home. Father was bringing her a new first reader, a new slate and a slate pencil to put in her knapsack. Boys and girls just starting to school ought always to have a new first reader, a new slate, and a slate pencil, Father said, because starting to school was special.

Just then Mother called up the stairs. "Hurry down, Bonnie, and wash your face and hands. It's twelve o'clock. Dinner is almost ready."

Bonnie left the window, lifted the knapsack from her shoulder, laid it on the bench, and smoothed all the wrinkles out of it. She unbuttoned the pink dress, pulled it over her head, hung it back carefully on the rod, and smoothed all the wrinkles out of it.

"Bon-nee!" came Mother's voice from downstairs.

"Coming!" called Bonnie as she jumped into her faded everyday dress, and ran down the stairs.

At the dinner table everyone talked about school.

"I'm going to finish my bat after dinner," said Chris. "Andy Watterson is making a ball. If we go to school early enough Monday morning, we can play a game of ball before the bell rings."

"I'm going to sit with Janie Sawyer," said Debby. "We planned it yesterday."

"Ellen Watterson and I are going to ask Miss Cora to let us erase the blackboards," said Emmy.

"I'm going to ask Miss Cora to let me ring the bell," said Chris.

"I'm going to ask Miss Cora to let me teach a class some day when she's busy," said Althy.

"What are you going to ask Miss Cora to let you do, Bonnie?" asked Mother.

"Everything," said Bonnie.

"You can't do everything the first day, Bonnie," laughed Debby. "It takes till Christmas to do everything."

"It takes a long time to do some things for Miss Cora," Althy said. "You can't teach a class for her until you're thirteen, like me."

"I wish we went to school every day," said Emmy. "I wish school didn't stop at Christmas."

"How would you get to school after Christmas?" asked Chris. "In January and February the snow would be up to your neck, and any day in March and April the rains might wash away the footbridge while you're at school, and how would you get home that night?"

"During the summer Father needs your help in the fields, and I need your help in the house, getting ready for winter," Mother reminded Emmy.

"Well, anyway," sighed Emmy, "I'm glad school starts in August."

To Bonnie, the afternoon seemed to drag more slowly than the morning. She dried the dishes for Althy. She waded in the river with Debby, and tried to catch minnows in her cupped hands, and watched crawfishes scuttling backwards among the pebbles. She sat in the kitchen and watched as Emmy pressed the new dress Mother had just finished for her. And she went fishing with Chris. But the time passed very slowly.

When the hands of the clock said four, Bonnie went again to the doorstep to watch for Father. The afternoon was sultry and still. Away off over the meadow a hawk circled and swooped. A yellow jacket flew past, and darted into his gray paperlike house glued to a branch of an apple tree. Down in the orchard an apple fell with a dull thud. And along the river road came the sound of a horse trotting.

Bonnie sat upright. It couldn't possibly be Father coming home, she thought. It was three long hours till sundown.

The sound of the trotting drew nearer.

Bonnie stood up. She gazed down the road as far as she could see. She ran to the gate, and climbed on it so that she could see farther still. As she watched, around the bend trotted Mag. On her back rode Father. Across the saddle lay a bundle.

"Here comes Father! Father's coming!" shouted Bonnie, like an alarm clock waking everybody up.

The Fairchilds came hurrying—Althy and Chris, Emmy and Debby. Mother came too. They crowded around as Father opened the bundle on the porch.

To Althy, Father handed big new books, an armful of them. To Chris and Emmy and Debby he handed new, long, brown pencils exactly alike, and new tablets, each with a different picture on the front.

"You'd better cut your initials on those pencils right away," said Father, "so you won't get them mixed up."

Last of all he handed Bonnie a new first reader, a new slate, and a new slate pencil. The book was crisp and clean, the slate hadn't a mark on it, and the pencil was long and gray and rounded at the end.

Bonnie stood holding them a minute. She wanted to thank Father, but she was so pleased she couldn't say a word. She could only swallow.

"I'll write your name in your book, Bonnie," offered Althy.

"I want Father to write my name," said Bonnie. And Father wrote, "This book belongs to Bonnie."

"I'll cut a B on your slate for you," offered Chris.

"Mother can make the best B," said Bonnie. "I want her to cut it." And Mother borrowed Father's knife and cut a B on the frame of Bonnie's slate.

"I'll carry your book upstairs when I take my tablet and pencil," offered Emmy.

"I can take it myself, thank you," said Bonnie. She tucked the first reader under her arm and held it tightly.

Chris watched her. "You'd think nobody ever had a book before," he said.

"I never had a book before," Bonnie told him.

Debby opened the book a crack and peeped inside. "Oh, look!" she cried. "There's Chicken Licken! I'll read it to you, Bonnie. Want me to?"

Bonnie thumbed through the book. True enough, there was Chicken Licken running for his life in fear that the sky might fall on him. Farther on Bonnie caught sight of the wolf huffing and puffing at the little pig's house. Farther still, Goldilocks was falling sound asleep in Baby Bear's bed.

Bonnie closed the book tightly. "I can read it myself," she said.

She carried the book, the slate, and the pencil upstairs and put them in her knapsack. Then she slung the knapsack across her shoulder. Wherever she went for the rest of the day, the knapsack with the book, the slate and the pencil inside, went with her.

At sundown, when she went with Althy to the mountain pasture to bring home the cows, the knapsack went too. When she carried in stovewood for Mother, she slung the knapsack on her back so that it would not get dirty. She ate supper with the knapsack in her lap.

When Bonnie was getting ready for bed, she took the book, the slate and the pencil out of the knapsack, and looked at them. With the pencil she made one long white mark on the slate. She thumbed through the book until she found Chicken Licken running for his life in fear that the sky might fall on him.

Then she put everything back in the knapsack, laid the knapsack beside her pillow, and got into bed.

She went to sleep singing softly in the dark a song she made for herself:

"Just one more day till Monday morning,
 One more day till Monday."

Whose Tree Is This?

As the sun poked its rim up over the mountains on Monday morning, it saw Althy and Chris, Emmy and Debby, and Bonnie, hurrying down the river road to school.

Chris was in front, whistling as he walked barefoot in the dusty wagon tracks. He carried his books under one arm and his hickory bat over his shoulder. Althy and Emmy and Debby came next, wearing their new dresses, and carrying their books under their arms. Emmy and Debby were barefoot, but Althy wore her new shoes. Althy carried the lunch pail too, and on top of her books was the Christmas play.

Last of all came Bonnie, wearing the pink dress on which Mother had embroidered a B. Her light hair was braided in two tight braids and tied with pink ribbons to match her dress. Across her shoulder was slung the knapsack.

"Don't walk so fast, Chris," Emmy called. "Bonnie can't keep up."

"Yes, I can keep up, too," said Bonnie. And she began to walk faster. The dust along the road felt warm and soft between her toes.

At the crossroads the Sawyers waited for them. At the bend in the road waited the Huffs.

"I have a new first reader," Bonnie called to Mary Huff, who was also going to school that day for the first time.

"So have I!" said Mary.

"Let's sit together," said Bonnie.

On down the road through the woods they went, Bonnie and Mary behind the others. At the footbridge the Wattersons waited for them.

"Hey, Andy!" shouted Chris. "Did you make that ball?"

For answer, Andy took a ball from his pocket. It was made of string, wound tightly and smoothly.

"See?" said Andy, holding the ball up. "It took me two whole days to make that."

"I'm going to be the first to bat," said Debby as they crowded around to feel how hard and firm Andy's ball was.

"We have to choose sides first," said Andy. "Chris made the bat and I made the ball, so we get to choose."

"We can choose before school starts if we hurry," said Chris.

He started running across the footbridge with Andy at his heels. Everybody ran but Bonnie and Mary Huff. Mary had to hold to the cables along the sides of the bridge. Bonnie walked very carefully, but she didn't hold to the cables.

Beyond the bridge the road ambled beside the river, through thickets of willow and clumps of yellow touch-me-nots. After a while it turned sharply into the woods. At the end of it stood the schoolhouse in a grove of oak trees. Deep woods skirted the east edge of the playground too, and continued down hollows and over hills and up into the far mountains where they looked blue like a frosty blue plum instead of green.

On the other two sides of the playground ran
an old rail fence, and beyond the fence butterflies and bees flitted and hovered among the tall
grasses and the frills of Queen Anne's lace grow-
ing in the meadow.

The door to the schoolhouse and all the windows were open wide, but no one was inside.
They were all on the playground, back of the
schoolhouse, watching while Chris threw his new
bat to Andy, and the two boys stacked their
hands on the bat to see who should have first
choice.

Miss Cora was on the playground too, standing where she could look straight through the

open window on one side of the schoolhouse to the open door on the other side, and down the road. When she saw Bonnie and Mary coming, she left the playground and waited for them at the door of the schoolhouse.

"Good morning, Bonnie and Mary," she said. "I was watching for you."

"This is the first time I have ever been to school," Mary told her.

"I know," said Miss Cora.

"I've been to school once," Bonnie said. "Once I came with Debby."

"I remember," said Miss Cora.

"But I didn't have a book that day," said Bonnie. "Now I have a book."

"I have a book too," said Mary.

"Let me show you your desk where you may put your books," said Miss Cora. "Then you will have time to play a few minutes before the bell rings."

The morning sun swept across the schoolroom, making everything clean and neat. It fell on Miss Cora's desk in the front of the room on which lay the Christmas play Althy had brought her. It lighted the bouquet of red cardinal flowers Margy Sawyer had picked for her beside the

river, tipping the tall spires with fire. It slanted across the blackboard on which Miss Cora had written the morning song. It shone on the desks —the big desks in the back of the room for the big girls and boys, and the little desks in the front of the room for the younger ones.

"Here is your desk, girls," said Miss Cora, pointing to the front desk in the row in which the girls sat. "And at this front desk in the boys' row, our other two first graders, Jimmy Sawyer and Davy Watterson, will sit."

Bonnie took her first reader and her slate from the knapsack and laid them on the desk. At the back of the desk she laid her slate pencil in the groove made especially for slate pencils. She folded her knapsack neatly and put it in the desk. Mary put her things away too. Then they went to the playground, leaving Miss Cora arranging things on her desk.

The ball game had begun. Debby was at bat. and Andy was pitching. The biggest Sawyer boy, Bob, was at first base, Althy was at second, and Margy Sawyer was at third. The biggest Huff boy was catching. Emmy was in the outfield. Chris and the other boys and girls were waiting their turn at bat.

Debby was swinging the bat, getting ready to hit the ball.

Bonnie and Mary edged across the outfield, past Emmy, past Althy at second base, and toward Bob Sawyer at first.

They stopped to watch Andy wind his arm to pitch the ball.

"Whack!"

Debby hit the ball and sent it flying just over first base. Bob Sawyer, running backwards to catch it in his cupped hands, tripped over Bonnie, the ball went rolling across the playground, and Debby, racing like a young colt, made a home run.

"Hey, Bonnie! You and Mary!" shouted Andy. "See what you've done! Get off the playground, you two!"

"We came to play," Bonnie called back.

"You're too little to play," Chris told them. "Nobody can play a ball game with first graders in it."

"Jimmy Sawyer and Davy Watterson are playing," said Bonnie, spying the two boys among the batters, near the home base.

"They're just watching," said Chris.

"Anyway, they're boys," said Andy. "You can

watch too, if you want to. But stand off in the woods out of the way."

Bonnie didn't like the idea of watching from the woods. But when she saw Andy winding his arm to pitch the ball again, and Chris swinging his bat to strike at it, and when she saw the hard ball speeding in her direction once more, she and Mary turned and ran to the edge of the woods to safety. She hadn't realized that the big boys in school were so big, nor that they could run so fast without looking where they were going.

When Miss Cora came to the door to ring the bell, the big boys thundered past Bonnie like stampeding horses, making her feel very small and frightened.

Emmy ran past too.

"When I was in first grade," she slowed down to say to Bonnie, "I played over there in the far corner of the playground under that big oak tree, out of the way of the ball game."

"I did too," said Debby, hurrying along out of breath from making a home run.

When the boys and girls had found their seats and the shuffling of feet had died down, Miss Cora called the roll. "Every morning," she said when the last one answered to the roll call, "before we begin our work, we shall sing."

Bonnie glanced at the big boys in the back of the room. What did it matter if they could run like runaway horses, she thought. She could sing as well as they. She could sing from daylight to dark and hardly finish all the songs Althy had taught her when they went for the cows at sunset.

She smoothed her pink dress carefully. Miss Cora tapped the bell. Together the boys and girls stood in the aisle and sang the song Miss Cora had written on the blackboard.

"Twenty froggies went to school,
Down beside a rushy pool.
Twenty little coats of green,
Twenty vests all white and clean.
'We must be on time,' said they,
'First we study, then we play.
That is how we keep the rule,
When we froggies go to school.'"

The singing over, the lessons began. To the tapping of the bell, the first graders sat erectly in their seats, rose, and marched to the long recitation bench in the front of the room. On the first page of their brand-new books they began to learn words about Chicken Licken. After the lesson they went back to their seats to draw pictures of Chicken Licken on their slates.

Soon, however, Bonnie laid her slate pencil in its groove and sat back in her seat to listen. She listened to the second graders and the third graders read stories from their books. She listened to Debby, she listened to Emmy, and she listened to Chris and Andy. Finally she listened to Althy as she read aloud from her reader a story about a shipwrecked man named Gulliver who made his home with little men the size of a green bean.

Bonnie sighed happily. School was like a storybook, she decided. School was like the biggest storybook in the world, and it would go on and on, story after story, until she had heard every story that had ever been told.

Just then Miss Cora tapped the bell, and the stories were over for that day.

Andy grabbed his ball, Chris raced to his bat, and the other boys and girls rushed to their places on the ball diamond. But Bonnie and Mary Huff skipped across the far end of the playground where balls never went, to the big oak tree that stood in the corner with the old rail fence just beyond it.

"Let's build a playhouse," suggested Bonnie.

"Here between these roots," agreed Mary.

"We can build it of sticks, like a log cabin," said Bonnie.

Just then Davy Watterson and Jimmy Sawyer

ran over to the tree to see what they were doing.

"You can build a better playhouse of rocks," said Davy when they told him their plans. "One time I built a rock playhouse big enough to get into. It had an upstairs and a downstairs. I could get in the upstairs, too."

"Let's build a playhouse big enough for all four of us to get into," suggested Bonnie.

"There are lots of rocks across the fence in the meadow," said Jimmy Sawyer. "I'll beat you to them."

Over the rail fence they tumbled. Until the bell rang they roamed over the meadow hunting smooth, flat stones and piled them beside the fence.

At noon time after they had eaten their lunch
with the other boys and girls, Jimmy Sawyer
climbed the fence and handed the rocks, one at
a time, to Mary and Bonnie, who carried them
to Davy under the trees.

"We'll need a pile of rocks as high as the fence
to build the house." Davy told them. "But we
can begin building the walls with what we have.
Tomorrow we can find some more."

Davy placed the rocks carefully, one on top
of the other. Slowly the walls of the playhouse
began to rise.

The first bell rang. It had a special meaning.

"Put away your ball and bat, boys and girls, and leave your playhouse, first graders," it ding-donged. "Get your drink of water and be ready to come in and study when the next bell rings."

The big boys and girls finished their ball game. Instead of going to the well for a drink of water, however, they ran to the big oak tree.

"What's that you're building?" asked Andy.

"A playhouse," they told him.

"Whew!" whistled Chris. "You must be building it for me. It's big enough for me to sleep in."

"It's big enough for both of us to sleep in," said Andy. "You crawl into that side, Chris, and I'll sleep on this."

"No, you can't, either!" stormed the four first graders.

"Andy and Chris are only teasing, children," said Miss Cora who had come to see what all the noise was about. "No one is going to bother your house, and no one may play here but you. This is your tree. But it's time to come in now. Chris, you may run and ring the bell."

When scarcely an hour had passed, Miss Cora tapped her bell. She was going to tap it at that time every day, she said. It meant that the first graders might go out for a special playtime of their own. But they must play quietly, she said. The older boys and girls who were having their lessons must not be disturbed.

Out the open door and across the playground to the big oak tree they hurried. Their heads were together as they built the walls of their playhouse, and when they talked it was like the buzzing of four bees in a sunny patch of clover.

"I'm going to bring some boards tomorrow for the upstairs floor."

"I can bring some for the roof."

"I can bring some too."

"We can carpet the floors with moss."

"Oh! Then our whole house will look like our parlor."

"I know where pretty moss grows."

"I saw some in the woods this morning. Close to the river."

"I'm going to make some furniture out of cornstalks tonight."

"My father can make little chairs and beds and tables that look just like real chairs and beds and tables."

"My father made an organ out of cornstalks one time."

"We can make dishes out of mud."

"We can use acorn cups for bowls."

"And big bur oak acorn cups for water buckets."

"I'm going to be the father."

"I'm going to be the mother."

"I want to be the mother."

"Why don't we take turns? You be the mother one day and I'll be the mother the next."

"All right. And the boys can take turns being the father."

Away they worked. The August sun was hot on the meadow, but the shade of the big oak tree was dim and cool. The playground was still in every corner except for the quiet hum of voices under the tree.

This special playtime was the best part of school, Bonnie was thinking as she helped build the wall. Well, maybe it wasn't better than the stories. But it was just as good.

"Querk-querk-querk-quee-ee-ee! Querk-quee-ee-ee! Quee-ee-ee-ee!" scolded a squirrel from the branches overhead.

"Look at him!" whispered Davy. "There on the second limb."

"He says, 'What are you doing here, first graders? This is my tree,' " laughed Bonnie.

"Look up there in the crotch of the tree!" said Mary. "He's building a house too."

"Querk-quee-ee-ee! Querk! Querk! Quee-ee-ee!" complained the squirrel. He flicked his handsome plumed tail at them. He jumped to another branch. He jumped back again. "Querk-quee-ee-ee!" he scolded.

"And look! Away up high!" whispered Mary Huff. "I see a bird's nest."

"But the eggs hatched long ago," Davy told her. "The birds aren't there."

"Knock-k-k-k-k-k-k!"

"Listen! A woodpecker!" whispered Jimmy.

The first graders peered into the dark green crown of the tree. High on the trunk they spied a red head bobbing madly.

"Maybe he has a house in this tree too," whispered Bonnie.

"Look!" whispered Davy excitedly. "Here's something else living in this tree."

"Where?" whispered Bonnie.

"On the bark," said Davy. "Right in front of you."

The flat grayish-brown head of a lizard was peeping around the tree trunk at them. Two bright eyes stared at them.

Bonnie inched her finger along the bark of the tree toward him. He turned and fled.

"This tree belongs to lots of people," laughed Bonnie.

Chris came to the door just then and rang the bell for the first graders to come in.

They left their playhouse and started across the playground.

"Querk-querk-quee-ee-ee!" fussed the squirrel as he watched them go.

"Knock-k-k-k-k-k-k-k-k!" madly pecked the woodpecker.

Somewhere among the dark branches a tree toad warbled a string of sore-throated noises, halfway between a croak and a purr.

The lizard scampered around the tree trunk and spied on them from the other side.

"Take good care of our tree," Bonnie called to them over her shoulder. "We'll be right back."

EVERY DAY the walls of the playhouse grew higher. Finally the house was finished. The floors were carpeted with moss. A cornstalk table and chairs and a cornstalk organ stood downstairs, and cornstalk beds stood upstairs. Every day the first graders played happily under the tree, and with their four heads together they buzzed like four bees in a sunny patch of clover.

Every day Bonnie tried to decide which was better—the playhouse, the special first-grade recess, the stories to which she listened every morning, or the story of Chicken Licken which she was learning to read from her own book. One morning when Miss Cora brought to school a cage she had made of very fine screen wire, Bonnie discovered she liked this best of all.

The cage was box-shaped, with a board for a floor, and a door in one end.

"What's it for?" the first graders asked as they crowded around Miss Cora.

"It's to put things in," explained Miss Cora. "I want you to bring something to live in it."

"Something alive?" asked Davy Watterson.

"Something wild?" asked Bonnie.

"Something that crawls?" asked Jimmy Sawyer.

"Something that flies?" asked Mary Huff.

"Something alive," said Miss Cora. "Something wild. It may run or crawl or fly or walk. Look for something as you come to school across the fields or through the woods. The woods and the fields are full of wild things. Whole families sometimes live on a single blade of grass. Whenever you walk through the woods, bright eyes are looking at you from almost every tree, and whenever you step, you may be stepping on somebody's house. Tomorrow," added Miss Cora, "Davy Watterson may bring something for our cage."

The next morning Davy Watterson came running through the woods with his hands cupped tightly.

"I've got something, Miss Cora!" he shouted when he was still a long way off. "Open the cage door and let me put him in. He's crawling around in my hands. Ouch, he tickles!"

Bonnie ran and opened the cage door. Everybody crowded around to see. Davy held his hands to the cage door, opened them, and out flew a ladybug. Bonnie slammed the door shut.

Then it was eight o'clock, and time for Chris to ring the bell. At once the ladybug set out to explore the cage.

When the first graders finished reading their lesson, they drew pictures of the ladybug on their slates. Bonnie drew a ladybug as big as her hand. She made thirteen spots on his wings. She gave him three pairs of long, crooked legs, and a pair of short, crooked feelers.

At recess the first graders fastened twigs inside the ladybug's cage. Then they watched him as he crawled over and under the leaves and up and down the twigs.

"He's trying to find his home," said Bonnie.

"Ladybugs haven't any home," Miss Cora said. "They are always on the go."

They left the ladybug in the cage when they went home that night. The next morning when Jimmy Sawyer opened the cage door to put a fresh twig inside, the ladybug spread his tiny, orange-colored wings and flew straight out the open window.

Until eight o'clock, when the bell rang, the first graders looked for him. Over and over they chanted:

> "Ladybug, ladybug,
> Fly away home.
> Your house is on fire,
> And your children do roam!"

But the ladybug never flew back. Miss Cora said he would be safe, however. He would fly into the woods, she said, and when winter came on he would crawl down under the dry leaves where it was warm, and stay until spring. When his work was done in the spring, he would die.

"Jimmy Sawyer may bring something for our cage tomorrow," Miss Cora said.

The next morning Jimmy Sawyer hurried to school carrying something in his cap.

"Open the cage door!" he shouted when he was still a long way off. "So I can put him in!"

Bonnie ran and opened the door. Jimmy held his cap close. Out tumbled a Daddy Longlegs. When he could straighten out his eight tangled legs, Daddy Longlegs ran as fast as he could into a corner. With the middle part of his long legs high in the air, and his little body swung low between them, he looked as if he were walking on four pairs of stilts.

The first graders drew his picture on their slates. At recess they went to the woods to hunt food for him. Miss Cora said he especially liked baby spiders and little insects.

But Daddy Longlegs wanted to find his own lunch. When he saw that Mary Huff had forgotten to shut the door tight, he scampered out of the cage. As the children came out of the woods, Bonnie caught sight of Daddy Longlegs

hurrying down the wall and under the school-house, his long stilt-like legs silvery in the sun.

They looked everywhere for him, but they couldn't find him.

"The day of the first hard frost, he will likely die," Miss Cora told them. "His work will be finished. Next spring you can find his children in the grass. Tomorrow Mary Huff may bring something for our cage."

The next morning Mary Huff came to school carrying a glass jar in her hands. Bonnie ran to open the door of the cage. Jimmy and Davy and Miss Cora came to watch.

Mary unscrewed the lid of the jar, and into the cage fluttered a beautiful big butterfly, all yellow and black, rimmed with blue, and trimmed with an orange ball on her hind wings.

"Oh!" sighed Bonnie. "She's pretty!"

"She is really beautiful," said Miss Cora. "She is all dressed up as if she were going to a party."

"Let's call her Cinderella," said Bonnie. And they did.

After their reading lesson, the first graders

drew Cinderella's picture on their slates. At recess they brought her twigs to rest on and a spike of goldenrod from which to sip nectar. When they went home at night they made sure the door of the cage was tightly shut so that Cinderella could not fly away.

But the next morning when they went to school, they found Cinderella lying quite still in a corner of the cage, her beautiful wings folded stiffly.

"Butterflies always die when their work is finished," Miss Cora told them. "But somewhere on the leaf of a tulip tree or a wild cherry leaf, Cinderella laid some eggs. You'll see her children next year. And now, Bonnie may bring something for our cage tomorrow."

The next morning on the way to school Bonnie loitered behind the others.

"Why don't you walk faster?" asked Chris. "We won't have time to play before the bell rings if you don't hurry."

"I'm looking for something special for the cage," said Bonnie.

"A bee?" asked Debby. "I see a bee."

"I don't want anything that flies," said Bonnie. "I want it to stay in the cage."

"A squirrel?" asked Emmy. "I see a squirrel."

"I don't want anything that runs fast," said Bonnie.

"Another butterfly?" asked Althy. "We could find another butterfly."

"I don't want anything that dies so quickly," said Bonnie. "I want something that lives a long time."

"Something that doesn't fly, doesn't run, and lives to be gray-headed. There isn't any such animal," said Chris.

"Anyway," said Bonnie, "I'm looking for one. You never can tell what you'll find in the woods. Miss Cora said so."

Down the road they went, Bonnie trudging barefoot behind the others, looking this way and looking that way for something wild.

At the crossroads the Sawyers waited for them.

At the bend in the road the Huffs joined them. And at the footbridge waited the Wattersons.

They were all on the footbridge before Bonnie reached it. At the bottom of the ramp she stood a minute looking in every direction, through the woods and up and down the river bank. She hoped to discover a little animal running through the grass, or hiding on the gray bark of a tree.

Suddenly she opened her eyes wide. Up the hill toward the path she saw exactly what she was looking for. It couldn't fly. It couldn't run. And though Bonnie had no idea how old it was, she was certain it was not going to die tomorrow.

She stood quietly in the path and waited. Closer and closer it ambled awkwardly on its four strong club feet. Its thick head was stuck far out of the brown-mottled house which it carried on its back. Its eyes were little and red. Up the hill it crawled—a big box turtle—and then straight across the path in front of Bonnie.

Bonnie reached down and touched the turtle with her finger.

Quick as a flash he pulled his legs inside his house.

In another flash he jerked in his leathery neck and his thick head.

46

"Hiss!" he said as he forced the air out of his lungs. Then he tightly locked his door.

Bonnie picked him up, took her first reader and her slate out of her knapsack and put the turtle in, then hurried to school.

"I've found something for the cage!" she shouted when she came in sight of the schoolhouse.

The boys and girls crowded around her, but Bonnie walked straight to the front of the schoolroom, put her hand in her knapsack, pulled out the turtle, and laid him on Miss Cora's desk.

"He is a very old turtle," said Miss Cora, picking him up and studying him. "He may be a hundred years old."

"Let's name him Grandpap," said Bonnie.

So they named him Grandpap.

It was not until Bonnie put him into the cage, shut the door, and went away that Grandpap finally opened the door of his house, and stuck out his thick head.

After their reading lesson, the first graders drew a picture of his mottled house, first with his feet and head outside of it, and then with his feet and head inside and the door shut.

Every morning the children brought Grand-

pap food—pawpaws they found in the woods
and ripe tomatoes from their gardens at home.
They caught flies for him, dug up leaf mold
in the woods and found long, fat earthworms
which he especially liked.

At first Grandpap only sat and stared at the
food as if he were saying a long grace.

"Your dinner is ready, Grandpap," said the
children, coaxing him to eat. Grandpap, however, ate his dinner when he pleased.

One day Bonnie offered Grandpap a bite of
muskmelon. He crawled up and nibbled it from
her hand. After that, every day he had muskmelon for dessert.

At recess the first graders took Grandpap out on the playground with them. When they played house, they let him sit in the corner in the sun and doze, since he was Grandpap. Sometimes they played "Chicky-ma-chicky-ma-craney-crow." Then they put Grandpap inside the circle and let him be the tender baby chicken whom they guarded from the old witch who was Mary Huff.

At noon they sometimes played "Whoopy-hide." Once they caught Grandpap crossing the bottom rail of the fence into the meadow. They shut their eyes until he was out of sight. Then they climbed the fence, ran and found him in the grass, and brought him back again.

Every day after that they played "Whoopy-hide" with Grandpap. Sometimes he walked about in the sun. Sometimes he dozed, his head halfway out of his house. Sometimes he sat and sulked, shut tightly in his house.

One bright day in late September when Grandpap was ambling about, warmed by the sun, the first graders shut their eyes and told him to run and hide.

When they thought he had had time to get away, they ran to look for him. They looked all around the tree. But Grandpap was not there.

They looked along the rail fence, but Grandpap was not there.

They climbed the fence and looked in the meadow. But Grandpap was not there.

They looked along the edge of the woods, scuffing their toes in the leaves and prodding with sticks around the roots of trees. But Grandpap was nowhere to be seen.

Then everybody set to looking for Grandpap. In and out of fence corners, up and down the playground, across the meadow and through the woods they went, looking and calling. But nowhere was there a sign of Grandpap.

"Has he gone off to die?" asked Bonnie. Tears stung her eyes.

"Not Grandpap!" said Miss Cora. "He's gone to find a sunny patch of woods where he can dig himself a deep hole and go to sleep for the winter. In the spring, when the days are long and really warm, you'll come across an old log some day, and there will be twenty turtles on it. One of them will be Grandpap."

"But how will I know which is Grandpap?" asked Bonnie.

Miss Cora puzzled about this a minute.

"He'll be the first on the log, I think," she said. "Because, you see, that's where Grandpap belongs."

A Day of Surprises

EVERY DAY for a week the first graders looked for Grandpap when they went to play, hoping that in spite of what Miss Cora had said, he might come plodding into their playhouse for another game of "Whoopy-hide." But Miss Cora was right. Grandpap never came back.

"We'll never have so much fun again as we had playing with Grandpap," Bonnie said sadly to Mother on Friday.

"Nonsense!" said Mother. She was hurrying about the kitchen getting breakfast ready. "Little girls are often mistaken. You're going to have fun this very day."

"What am I going to do?" asked Bonnie.

"I have a surprise for you," said Mother. "I'll tell you when you're ready for breakfast."

Bonnie brought the comb to Althy and stood as still as she could while Althy combed and braided her light hair. Althy made tiny braids back of Bonnie's ears, and two braids not much bigger than a pencil in the back. She tied the ends of the braids with ribbons of pink cloth like Bonnie's pink dress embroidered with a B.

Tears swam in Bonnie's eyes as Althy combed
and braided. Usually Bonnie complained. "Ouch,
Althy! You're skinning me alive!" she usually
said. That morning, however, she only sneezed
and said nothing, so that Althy might hurry, and
Mother might tell her what the surprise was.

"Ready, Mother," said Bonnie, when Althy
tied the last ribbon.

"How would you like to ask Miss Cora to
spend the night with us?" Mother asked.

"Oh, let me ask her!" begged Emmy.

"I'm going to ask her," said Debby.

"Mother said I could ask her," Bonnie said.
"Debby has asked her once, anyway."

"Debby asked her last year," said Mother. "And Emmy asked her the year before that. So Bonnie may ask her this year. And tell her, Bonnie," she added, "that we're going to do something special."

"We're going pawpaw hunting," guessed Emmy.

"You go pawpaw hunting every day on your way to school," laughed Mother.

"We're going grape hunting," guessed Debby.

"It's too early to hunt grapes," said Mother. "Jack Frost hasn't sweetened them yet."

"We're going . . . we're going . . . we're going persimmon hunting!" guessed Bonnie.

"A persimmon now would screw your mouth as tight as Althy has drawn your hair," laughed Mother.

"Not even the possums are hunting persimmons yet," said Emmy.

"Not even if they were as hungry as Grandpap," said Debby.

"Then what is it, Mother?" asked Bonnie.

"If I tell you, it won't be a surprise," said Mother. "But you will like it. So will Miss Cora. So will everybody else."

A bright sun was peeping over the mountain

tops as they started down the road to school. It shone warmly on the hollow and on the river road. It spangled with silver the festooned spider webs, heavy with dew, swaying on the tall grasses. Debby stopped to look at them. She was going to draw a picture of them when she got to school, she said. But Bonnie hurried on.

When they passed under the chestnut tree at the edge of the mountains, Emmy and Chris stopped to see if any prickly burrs had fallen. Chris found one burr and Emmy two. But Bonnie didn't look for burrs. She hurried on.

On a mountainside meadow Althy picked a

bunch of purple meadow stars to take to Miss Cora. Almost every morning Bonnie found something to take to Miss Cora—an oak gall, a lacy fern, or a ghostly Indian pipe. That morning, however, she hurried to school as fast as she could go, without looking to the left or the right.

She was the first to reach the schoolhouse, and at once she asked Miss Cora to spend the night with her.

Miss Cora said she could. She said too that she always liked spending the night at Bonnie's house.

"You'll like it more than ever tonight," Bonnie said. "We're going to do something special."

"May I guess what it is?" asked Miss Cora.

"It wouldn't do any good to guess," said Bonnie, "because, you see, I don't know myself."

It seemed to Bonnie that no school day had

ever been so long. She stood erect at her seat and sang with the other boys and girls:

"When Johnny Poole first went to school,
He was but scarcely seven;
But he knew as well how to read and spell
As most of the boys of eleven."

But she was glad when the song was finished.

The first graders were reading the story of Goldilocks and the three bears. Bonnie liked that even better than the story of Chicken Licken. But she was glad that day when Goldilocks ate all of Little Bear's mush and the reading lesson was over.

She was glad when Emmy finished reading about an ugly little duckling, even though she wished she knew the end of the story.

She didn't make a sound when Althy stood before the room and read a poem about a bobolink.

"Bob-o-link, Bob-o-link!
Spink! Spank! Spink!"

read Althy. Althy sounded so like a bird that for a moment Bonnie thought it was bobolink weather, and she was lying in the meadow with sun on her, with daisies and Queen Anne's lace swaying in the wind, and with huge white clouds sailing over her in a sea of blue. But she was glad when the poem ended and Althy quit being a bird.

All day Bonnie watched the shadows on the floor. In the morning they came from the windows on one side. In the afternoon they came from the windows on the other side. When the shadow of the big oak tree under which their playhouse was built reached Miss Cora's desk, it was time to go home.

Through the woods and across the footbridge they went—the Sawyers, the Huffs, the Wattersons, the Fairchilds, Althy and Chris, Emmy and Debby, and Bonnie walking proudly beside Miss Cora.

When they crossed the footbridge, the Wattersons left them. At the bend in the road the Huffs turned west. At the crossroads the Sawyers said good-bye.

Finally at sundown they came within sight of the house.

Chris climbed the bank beside the river road and looked for a surprise.

"I see it! I see it! I know what it is!" he shouted. He clambered down the bank, getting his pants very dirty as he did so. He broke into a run down the road. "I'll beat everybody home!" he called over his shoulder.

Debby raced him down the road.

Emmy climbed the bank and looked toward the house.

"I see it! I see it! Hurry, everybody!" she shouted. And away she ran after Chris and Debby.

Althy and Miss Cora and Bonnie climbed the bank and looked.

"I see it!" cried Althy. "I know what it is!"

"I see it too," said Miss Cora. "I was thinking it was the right time of year."

Bonnie looked and looked. But she couldn't see anything that surprised her. She tried to remember what ought to happen in October when the trees were fiery with color, when the days were bright with sun, and the nights with a hint of frost in them sparkled with stars. But she couldn't remember.

"Come on, Bonnie. Let's hurry," said Althy, climbing down the bank.

"Aren't you anxious to get home, Bonnie?" asked Miss Cora. She climbed down the bank too.

Bonnie was anxious to get home. But she was more anxious to find out what the surprise was. So she climbed to the top of the rail fence that stood on the bank and looked toward the house.

Then she saw what was happening.

In the woodlot a fire was burning under a long black pan. Father was unloading long green stalks of sorghum cane from the wagon, heaping them in a pile. Mag, hitched to a long beam, was walking slowly around, and around, and around, always in the same big circle. Andy Watterson's father was sitting on a log feeding the cane, heavy with juice, between two cogged rollers.

"Molasses making!" cried Bonnie.

She tumbled off the fence, and down the bank. She would have started running down the road. But since Miss Cora was walking, she walked too, until they reached the woodlot.

At the supper table Mother smiled at Bonnie who was sitting beside Miss Cora. "The surprises aren't over yet," she said. "As soon as we have finished supper, Bonnie, you may gather up all the teaspoons and bring them to the woodlot."

"Why do you want so many?" asked Bonnie.

"You'll see," said Mother.

In the woodlot after supper, Chris hitched Mag to the long beam again. Bonnie watched the little mare as she plodded around and around until the last stalk of cane had been ground, and the last drop of juice had trickled into the bucket underneath the rollers.

Then Debby climbed on Mag and rode her away to the pasture. Mr. Watterson emptied the juice into the long black pan. Chris stirred the fire. Father skimmed the juice with Mother's big kitchen spoon to which he had wired a pole for a handle. Bonnie passed out the teaspoons. She gave Miss Cora a special one.

The juice in the pan boiled and bubbled. Sweet steam rose from it. Carefully Father skimmed off the foam with his enormous spoon.

"May I have some now, Father?" asked Bonnie, holding her spoon under his big skimming spoon to catch the juice.

"It will taste better when it turns to gold," said Father. "If you'll look," he added, "I think you'll see another surprise at the gate."

Bonnie turned quickly. There stood all the Wattersons, all the Huffs, and all the Sawyers, come to the molasses making.

"Now you see why we needed so many spoons,
Bonnie," said Mother.

Each of the children took a spoon. They
crowded around the pan where Father was skimming the foam from the boiling juice, and held
their spoons under his long-handled spoon. Sometimes clouds of steam covered him. When the
children stood near, it covered them too. They
liked that. They sniffed and sniffed. The steam
smelled sweeter than sugar.

"It isn't molasses yet," said Bonnie, sipping
from her spoon.

"It won't be molasses for a long time," Father
told her.

"Why don't we play some games?" asked Miss Cora.

"Why don't we play 'Whoopy-hide'? In the dark?" asked Bonnie.

Andy Watterson hid his eyes at the woodlot gate. The others trooped away into the darkness to hide. One minute the woodlot echoed with whooping and yelling. The next minute, except for the crackling sound the fire made and the little sounds the fathers and mothers made as they sat about the fire talking, it was as still as the starry sky.

From far away came Chris' voice, loud and long and ringing. "Whoo-oo-oo-pee-hide!"

Bonnie crouched behind the sorghum mill. Miss Cora crouched beside her.

Footsteps went running past them—Andy's footsteps. Andy hunted and hunted. Sometimes he crept up so quietly in the dark that no one could hear him. Sometimes he went flying back to base when he saw someone. But he never found Chris. And once when he was a long way from base, Bonnie and Miss Cora ran home free.

They played three games of "Whoopy-hide." Then they gathered around the fire again and held their spoons underneath Father's big spoon to catch the hot drops of juice that were beginning to thicken now.

"It's almost molasses!" cried Bonnie.

"Not yet," said Father. "See?"

He lifted his skimming spoon. A stream of hot liquid, sweet and thick and golden, poured from it. "It has to turn red before it is molasses."

"Let's do something else," suggested Bonnie.

"Let's sing," suggested Althy.

Gathering in a circle about the fire, they sang all the songs they knew—school songs and camp meeting songs, and old, old love songs that have been sung in the mountains since Daniel Boone was a boy. Mother sang and Father sang. Mr. Watterson sang and Mrs. Watterson sang. Everybody sang.

"It's thickening now," called Father when they finished singing,

> *"There was a frog lived in the spring,*
> *Sing song Kitty can't you kimey O."*

The boys and girls crowded about the long pan, holding out their spoons. Their eyes smarted with smoke, and sweet steam blew into their faces. Over and over Father filled their spoons with the thickening molasses.

"Just a few minutes now and it will be done," said Father.

"Shall we sing 'Barbara Allen'?" asked Miss Cora.

They sang "Barbara Allen." And they sang "Chickens a-Crowing in the Sourwood Mountain." And they sang,

> *"One morning, one morning in the spring,*
> *I went to sea to serve my king."*

Bonnie, sitting beside Miss Cora, listened as the singing filled the woodlot, as it soared far up over the sweetgum tree and was lost among the stray sparks from Father's fire. The sweet smell of the molasses mingled with the cool air of the night.

Bonnie snuggled close to Miss Cora. Her eyes closed.

The singing, she thought, was . . . was filling the earth. . . . It was crowding . . . crowding against the stars in the wide blue sky.

"She's had such a long day!" Bonnie heard Miss Cora saying. "And such a happy one!" Her voice seemed to come from a long way off.

Somebody took Bonnie by the hand and helped her to her feet. "And she's so full of molasses!" laughed Mother.

Through the darkness toward the house they went, Mother leading the way, Bonnie stumbling sleepily behind.

"I don't want to go to bed, Mother," she fretted. "I don't want the surprise to end."

Mother waited while Bonnie washed her face and hands in the kitchen. Then she held the lamp to light Bonnie's way up the stairs to bed.

"The surprise isn't ending," said Mother. "It has only begun. Miss Cora is going to stay with us a whole week."

The Wind and the Leaves

IT SEEMED strange to Bonnie when the week was finally ended and Miss Cora was there no longer.

"I'm going to ask Miss Cora to spend another week with us," said Bonnie as they started to school on Monday morning. Late autumn sunshine was drenching the mountains and flooding the low hollows with gold. A tall wind was blowing.

"Miss Cora's going to spend a week with Mary Huff next," Debby told her.

The wind caught Debby's voice and carried it away. With it went racing golden leaves from the poplar trees and brown leaves from the sycamores, crimson leaves from the sumac and ruby red leaves from the sweetgum trees.

The wind tickled Debby's feet. She began to skip gaily down the road, singing as she skipped.

"I'm going to be buried today, today!
I'm going to be buried today!"

"Emmy," said Bonnie, "don't you think the

first graders could play 'Wild Animal'? I'm big enough to be buried."

"You wouldn't lie still enough, Bonnie," Althy said over her shoulder. "You have to lie as still as a Wild Animal Holed Up for the Winter."

"I wouldn't make a sound," promised Bonnie. "I'd scarcely get my breath."

"Shucks, you can't run fast enough, Bonnie," said Chris. "It's no fun playing unless the Wild Animal can run fast. You'd better stick to your playhouse."

"I can run faster than I could run this time last year," said Bonnie.

"You can run fast enough to catch Mary Huff," said Emmy. "And in a pinch you might catch Davy Watterson and Jimmy Sawyer."

Just then they were at the crossroads where the Sawyers were waiting for them, and Emmy did not have time to say whether she thought Bonnie might be buried in the leaves that day.

For over a week the big boys and girls had left their bat and ball in the schoolhouse, and had been playing "Wild Animal Holed Up for the Winter." It was their favorite game on fine autumn days when leaves were fluttering to the ground in great golden hordes, and the woods were mellow with sun. Every morning before the eight o'clock bell rang, they played it. They played it at every recess time, and every day at noon when they had eaten their lunch under the trees.

That morning, as soon as they reached school, Debby was chosen to be the Wild Animal.

"I'll bury her," said Margy Sawyer. "Come on, Debby."

Into the woods they ran while the other boys and girls stood on the far side of the schoolhouse with their eyes closed and their fingers in their ears.

Deep in the woods, Margy and Debby found a spot beside a poplar tree. Debby lay on her back on the ground and closed her eyes. Margy covered her with leaves. Then she ran back to the schoolhouse.

"Ready!" she shouted at the edge of the woods.

At once the others opened their eyes, took their fingers out of their ears, and scattered through the woods. They pretended to be hunting for chestnuts so that they would be surprised when a Wild Animal growled at them from a pile of leaves and chased them through the woods. But they were really hunting for Debby.

It took them a long time to find her, because

there were so many mounds of leaves about the woods through which they had to scuff before Andy Watterson scuffed into the mound where Debby was buried.

From underneath the leaves came a low, deep growl—as fierce a growl as Debby could growl.

"Help! Help!" shouted Andy as he started running through the woods. "A Wild Animal's after me!"

The other boys and girls began to run too.

After them ran Debby, with leaves in her hair, leaves in her shoes, and leaves clinging to her clothes. To the playground they raced, around

and around the schoolhouse, Debby after them,
growling fiercely as she chased them.

Just then Margy Sawyer came to the door and
rang the bell. All the boys and girls trooped into
the room and to their desks, panting so hard from
running that they scarcely had breath enough to
sing "Twenty Froggies."

At recess, Clarissy Huff was chosen to be the
Wild Animal.

At noon the boys and girls carried their lunch
pails onto the playground and sat under the trees
to eat. Bonnie ate her lunch very quickly. When
she finished, she whispered in Emmy's ear.

"Who's going to be the Wild Animal now?" asked Andy Watterson.

"Let Bonnie be the Wild Animal this time," said Emmy.

"She's never been a Wild Animal, has she?" asked Margy Sawyer.

"No," said Emmy. "And soon the burying season will be over. One day soon rain will begin to fall, and snow will fly through the woods, and we'll hunt no more Wild Animals."

"Bonnie won't be hard to find," said Chris. "If we hurry, we can find two Wild Animals before the bell rings."

"Come on, Bonnie," said Emmy, jumping up from the ground. "I'll bury you."

The other boys and girls closed their eyes and put their fingers in their ears.

Deep into the woods hurried Emmy, with Bonnie close behind her. Past a hundred leaf mounds they went, where other Wild Animals had lain in wait for boys and girls out hunting chestnuts in the woods, past the farthest mound where Margy Sawyer had hidden Debby that morning.

Still farther they went—across a fern-filled ravine and up to the top of a ridge where no

Wild Animal had ever hidden and where boys and girls never went hunting for nuts. Low twigs, bare of their leaves, snarled Bonnie's hair. Gold leaves, brown leaves, yellow leaves, red leaves whirled and dived and skipped before the wind.

"Where are we going, Emmy?" asked Bonnie.

"We're going far enough away to teach Chris a lesson," said Emmy. "It isn't going to be so easy to find you as he thinks."

High on the ridge they stopped under a beech tree. Its branches, gray as slate, were almost bare. Underneath, the ground was carpeted thickly with gold.

"This is a good place," said Emmy. "Lie down flat. And don't growl until somebody scuffs against you. I won't pile the leaves very high. Then you'll be harder to find."

Bonnie stretched flat on her back on the carpeted ground, and shut her eyes. Over her Emmy heaped little gold beech leaves, and big fan-shaped golden poplar leaves, and maple leaves red as an autumn fire.

"There, now!" said Emmy. "Don't wiggle a finger. We'll teach Chris a thing or two!"

She turned and ran down the slope and through the woods.

"Ready!" she called when finally she reached the schoolhouse. She was almost out of breath, for she had been running a long way.

Into the woods ran the boys and girls, all except Emmy and Ellen Watterson, who stayed behind to help Miss Cora. They erased the blackboard until it was black as night. They dusted the erasers. They put new, long pieces of chalk about the blackboard. They climbed the fence to the meadow and picked a bunch of purple meadow stars for Miss Cora's desk. Emmy was so busy that she forgot all about Bonnie.

High on the slope under the old gray beech tree Bonnie waited. She was so far from the schoolhouse that she couldn't hear when Emmy shouted "Ready!" She lay very still, scarcely making a sound with her breathing, as she listened for boys and girls to climb the slope hunting for nuts. She heard noises that might have been scuffing. She could not be sure. They might have been the wind that was romping and rollicking so boisterously among the leaves. She supposed she ought to practice growling.

"Gr-r-r-r!" she said, ever so softly. The wind lifted the gentle noise and lost it as it made off up the far haze-covered mountains.

It was warm and soft among the beech leaves. Bonnie opened her eyes a slit. Sunlight sifted through the thin leaf covering. The whole earth and the sky over it seemed turned to gold.

Quietly Bonnie lay listening, but nowhere could she hear feet scuffing in the leaves, nowhere could she hear Andy Watterson shouting to Chris. Only the branches of the great gray beech tree could she hear swaying and swinging and swishing in the wind.

With her fingers she pushed the leaves from her face and opened her eyes. Over the winding slope the tall wind blew. Over her the leaves went flying, skipping, dancing, reeling, tumbling, soaring, dipping, frolicking one last mad, golden frolic before the rains came to bed them down and the silent snow to cover them over.

Quietly Bonnie lay, watching.

A cardinal, red as the sumacs along the woods' edge, bobbed by on the wind and stopped on a bare branch directly over Bonnie. She could see his long gnarled toes curling tightly about the twig on which he perched. His proud crest gleamed handsomely in the sun. He cocked a bright eye at Bonnie, but he didn't see her. The twig on which he perched bobbed and swayed so low that once it almost swept the leaves that covered her. She could have reached out a finger and touched the bird. But not a muscle did she move. Once more the cardinal cocked his head and looked at her. Then he spread his wings and flashed away on the wind.

Quietly Bonnie lay.

Between gusts of wind she could hear little red haws dropping out of the haw tree that grew near by. "One. Two. Three. Four. Five," she counted as they dropped. Red haws dropping would certainly make Chicken Licken run for his life, she thought, because on such a windy day he would think the sky was falling and the whole earth was blowing away besides. But Bonnie lay quietly in the leaves. "Six. Seven. Eight. Nine. Ten. Eleven."

It was the pleasantest thing in the world to lie so long in the leaves with the wind blustering over her and the sun warming her, she thought. But it was taking Chris a long time to find her.

She looked up through the bare gray branches into the sky. It seemed to have no beginning, and no end. The swaying branches made dark patterns against the blue—swaying, moving patterns that came and went, came and went, rested and came and went.

Suddenly Bonnie discovered something. Far off in the blue sky a long, tapering V was moving. The big blue geese had felt the chilly winter wind blowing on them somewhere far to the North. They were hurrying toward warm marshes and reedy lakes in the South. Through the branches of the tree Bonnie watched them.

"Honk!" One note bugled from the sky, as clear as a bell. Then another, and another. "Honk! Honk! Honk!" Then, somewhere in the sky, the blue geese faded and were gone.

Quietly Bonnie waited a long, long time.

Suddenly she heard a scuffing. It was under the beech tree, quite near her. But it was such a tiny scuffing Bonnie didn't think it could be Chris.

Very, very quietly she turned her head and looked. Close to the tree trunk sat a gray squirrel holding an acorn in his forepaws and peeling it with his sharp teeth. He looked very comical spitting out the shells.

"Gr-r-r-r!" Bonnie growled at him gently.

He cocked his head slightly, snapped his teeth on the acorn, and scampered up the trunk of the beech tree for his life.

As Bonnie lay waiting she heard another scuffing. This one was farther away. But it was louder. It sounded like the scuffing of someone who is out hunting for nuts and is likely to disturb a Wild Animal Holed Up for the Winter.

Bonnie snuggled down in the leaves. She lay as still as snow lies on the ground.

Scuff. Scuff. Scuff.

Somebody was coming quite near—quite, quite near. It sounded like Chris.

The scuffing stopped.

"Bon-nee!"

Bonnie listened sharply. It wasn't Chris calling. It was Emmy. That was strange.

"Bon-nee! Where are you, honey?"

As still as the roots of the beech tree Bonnie lay under the leaves listening. Hadn't Emmy told her to wait until somebody scuffed against her?

Scuff. Scuff. Scuff. Nearer and nearer the scuffing came.

"Bon-nee-ee-ee! Answer me, honey. It's Emmy. I can't find where I buried you!"

Scuff. Scuff. Scuff. Nearer and nearer. *Scuff* right into the mound of leaves where Bonnie lay buried.

"GR-R-R-R!" growled Bonnie. Out of the leaves she bounded and pounced on Emmy.

"Oh, Bonnie!" cried Emmy. Her voice was half-scolding. "Why didn't you answer me?"

"You said not to answer until somebody scuffed against me," Bonnie told her. "Remember?"

"But didn't you know the game was over?" Emmy asked. "The bell rang long ago. Then everybody came inside and got busy with their lessons, and didn't notice you weren't there until Miss Cora said, 'Where's Bonnie? It's time for her arithmetic lesson.'"

They hurried down the slope, across the ravine, and through the woods toward the schoolhouse.

"I had a good time up there under the leaves," said Bonnie. "You can see more things when you lie on your back on the ground!"

"But I wish you had answered," said Emmy. "Miss Cora sent me to look for you, and I'd forgotten where I buried you. I've looked under every beech tree on the slope. I thought you were lost."

"If I had known, Emmy, I would have answered," said Bonnie. "The next time you call, I'll be sure to answer."

On they hurried, the wind blowing in their faces, their feet scuffing the crisp, newly fallen leaves.

"Miss Cora is waiting for you to count to fifty," said Emmy.

But Bonnie wasn't thinking about counting to fifty.

"Chris didn't find me, did he?" she said. "Now I can be the Wild Animal again tomorrow, can't I? Will you hide me in the very same spot, Emmy?"

Rain on the Windowpane

LITTLE by little, winter came. The ball and the bat stood untouched in a corner of the schoolroom. The playhouse under the oak tree was deserted. Every day the squirrel looked about and wondered where his companions were.

The day before Thanksgiving, morning dawned gray and sullen. At breakfast Mother looked out the window at the sky and said, if she was any judge of the weather, it was going to rain before night, and children should go to school prepared.

Althy and Chris, Emmy and Debby and Bonnie buttoned themselves into their warm winter coats, and Chris pulled his big rubber boots on his feet. Mother said Althy could take her little umbrella, and Emmy could take Father's big one.

"I'm going to walk with Althy," said Debby.

"I'm going to walk with Emmy," said Bonnie.

"Oh, I do hope it will rain," said Debby. "I like to walk under umbrellas!"

Down the road they went to school. At the crossroads the Sawyers were waiting for them.

Margy carried Mr. Sawyer's big black umbrella. It was big enough for all four of the Sawyers to stand under it without getting wet. Margy opened it up and the four Sawyers stood under it to show everybody.

When they rounded the bend in the road, they saw the three Huffs waiting for them.

"Where's your umbrella?" called Debby.

"We've got boots. See?" said Mary Huff. And the three Huffs displayed boots on their feet.

"Boots are better in case of snow," said Clarissy Huff. "And they're just as good as an umbrella in the rain. An umbrella doesn't keep your feet dry."

"I'd rather have my head dry," said Debby. "Give me an umbrella on a rainy day!"

At the footbridge the five Wattersons were waiting for them. They carried Mrs. Watterson's little black umbrella and Mr. Watterson's big black umbrella. But Andy needed no umbrella. He was wearing a shiny black raincoat that came down almost to his heels. He had boots on his feet and a rain hat on his head. "I don't care what kind of weather we have," he boasted, running across the footbridge. "I'm ready for anything."

Hardly were they inside the schoolhouse before the rain came. It started as a cold, dismal drizzle. Before Miss Cora said Chris might ring the bell, it had turned into a steady downpour.

The boys and girls sang their special Thanksgiving song that morning.

"To grandmother's house we go,
Heigh-ho! Heigh-ho!"

Their voices rang merrily. But louder than their voices was the sound of the drumming rain.

Bonnie looked out the window. Gray, slanting spears of rain pricked the windowpane. Sheets of water streamed over the glass. Rain fell so

fast and so hard that Bonnie could not see the nearest oak tree on the playground.

Inside the schoolhouse it was dark too. Miss Cora lighted the four lamps on the walls of the room.

The first graders went to the recitation bench. But it was too dark for reading.

"I wonder if Grandpap is keeping dry in his hole in the ground," said Davy Watterson.

"Very dry," said Miss Cora.

"I wonder if he is keeping warm," said Bonnie.

"Warm as mittens," said Miss Cora. She told Chris to put more coal in the big stove that stood in the middle of the room.

"Let it rain and blow as hard as it pleases," she said. "We shall be warm as mittens too."

"Will the rain stop at recess?" asked Bonnie.

"Maybe," said Miss Cora.

But the rain had not stopped at recess. It was still pelting the windowpanes, still drumming on the roof.

"No more hunting Wild Animals Holed Up for the Winter," said Emmy.

"No more playing ball," said Andy Watterson. "For a whole year."

"No more playhouse," said Bonnie.

"No more playing 'Chicky-ma-chicky-ma-craney-crow,'" said Mary Huff.

"Nor 'Whoopy-hide,'" said Davy Watterson.

"There are all sorts of games for all sorts of days," said Miss Cora. "And today is a guessing game day."

She began pulling the desks in a circle around the stove. The boys and girls helped her.

"Let's play 'Guess My Pretty Bird's Name!'" suggested Debby.

Miss Cora made a little cup of paper, the size

of a thimble. Davy Watterson was chosen to be
It. He filled the cup with water, and went around
the circle, asking, "Guess my pretty bird's name."

Debby guessed a dove. Clarissy Huff guessed a
bluebird. Andy guessed a chimney sweep. Chris
guessed a sharp-billed hawk. Margy Sawyer guessed
a buzzard. Althy guessed a wren. Emmy guessed
a mocking bird. Bonnie guessed a woodpecker,
and *splash!* The little cup of water landed in her
face, for the red-headed woodpecker in the big
oak tree was the bird Davy was thinking of.

Then Bonnie was It. She filled the cup with
water and went around the circle asking, "Guess
my pretty bird's name."

The boys and girls guessed and guessed. They guessed all the birds that fill the woods and the fields with bird song—the owl and the meadow lark, the robin and the cardinal, the peewee and the thrush, the brown thrasher and the bobolink, the bobwhite and the mocking bird and the warbler. But to all of these Bonnie shook her head.

They guessed all the birds they had read about in their books—the pelican and the coot, the prairie chicken and the passenger pigeon, the cormorant and the flamingo, the stork and the curlew and the condor and the ostrich. But to all of these Bonnie shook her head.

"A wild goose!" guessed Althy. And *splash!* Bonnie threw the water in Althy's face, because she was thinking of the big blue geese that flew high in the sky when she was buried in the leaves.

Then recess was over, but the rain was still pelting the windowpanes, still drumming noisily on the roof.

At twelve o'clock it was still raining. The boys and girls brought their lunch pails and sat in a circle about the stove to eat.

"Remember when we were studying about floods in our geography, Miss Cora?" asked Althy.

"Everything washes away in floods—houses and barns, and cattle and horses and cats and dogs, and whole fields of corn and wheat."

Althy brought her geography and showed the boys and girls the pictures of the flood. Housetops were swirling in the muddy water like the paper boats Emmy dropped into the river from the footbridge.

"If you had a boat you'd be safe in a flood," said Chris.

"Let's play 'If I Had a Boat,'" said Debby. "We can tell where we would like to go in a boat."

So they sat around the stove and played "If I Had a Boat." They looked at the map in Althy's geography, and, starting at the footbridge, they rowed down little rivers to big rivers, and down big rivers out to the open sea. And they went to far-away places that Bonnie had never heard of— the Baltic Sea and the Black Sea, the China Sea and the Japan Sea, the Java Sea and the North Sea, the Coral Sea and the Sea of Marmara.

Chris put more coal in the stove. Bonnie walked to the window and looked out.

"Come and look!" she called. "Miss Cora, come and look! We don't have to start our boats at the footbridge. The schoolhouse is in the middle of a sea."

The boys and girls crowded to the windows. Though rain was still falling, the sky was lighter. And as Bonnie had said, water was standing everywhere about the schoolhouse.

But Miss Cora didn't seem at all disturbed. "Shall we play 'Bird, Beast, or Fish' the rest of the noon hour?" she asked.

Bonnie, however, was disturbed. As she sat by the stove and played "Bird, Beast or Fish," she thought how fearful a thing it would be to see a schoolhouse go floating down a muddy river and out to the Coral Sea.

At the afternoon recess the rain had slowed to a drizzle.

"Andy," said Miss Cora, "suppose you and Chris put on your boots, and go down the road to see how high the river is."

At once Andy and Chris set out. They shouted and laughed, they ran and stamped, they whooped and hollered as they went down the road. Their boots swished in the water, and made great splashes with every step.

It seemed to Bonnie a long time before they came back. Margy Sawyer was reading a story from her reader when Chris burst into the door with Andy at his heels.

"The footbridge has washed away, Miss Cora!" shouted Chris.

"This end of it has washed loose," panted Andy.

"The bridge is in the middle of the river," said Chris. "We can't get home tonight."

The boys and girls crowded around Andy and Chris, asking questions. Mary Huff began to cry.

"What will we do for our supper, Miss Cora?" Jimmy Sawyer asked. He began to cry too.

"Where will we sleep?" asked Davy Watterson. He looked very solemn, as if he might be going to cry.

Bonnie looked at Miss Cora. She felt very much like crying. But Emmy wasn't crying. Nor Debby. No one was crying but Mary Huff and Jimmy Sawyer, who wanted his supper.

"Come and sit down, boys and girls," said Miss Cora. "We'll have no more lessons today. We'll do something special."

They took their seats about the stove.

"A long time ago Althy brought a Christmas play for our last day of school," said Miss Cora. "I meant to wait until after Thanksgiving to begin practicing it. But we'll begin today. While we're gathered about the stove, I'll read the play to you."

The boys and girls grew quiet, and Miss Cora began to read.

Bonnie nestled close to Emmy to listen. She forgot about the rain. She forgot about the footbridge in the middle of the river. She was thinking of the good farmer and his wife in the play, and of their seven children with whom they lived in a little farmhouse at the edge of a meadow. She was thinking of the farmer's cattle, and of the

extra fodder the farmer fed them on the eve of Christmas. She was thinking of the steaming Christmas broth the farmer's wife was cooking over the hearth fire. She was thinking of the lame boy Peter who opened the door for the tired old man who was lost on Christmas Eve, and of Elsa who first saw the Christmas angel coming across the starlit meadow. And especially was she thinking of the Christmas angel.

When Miss Cora was on the last page of the play, Bonnie heard a noise down the road. Turning toward the window, she saw coming through the rain toward the schoolhouse a wagon pulled by two horses, dripping wet. In the seat

sat the driver bundled to his ears in a wet slicker, his dripping hat pulled down over his eyes.

"Father!" cried Bonnie. "Here comes Father!"

"Yes, it's time to go home now," said Miss Cora. "Get your things quickly, boys and girls."

Father drove the wagon right up to the door of the schoolhouse, and everybody climbed in— the Wattersons, the Huffs, the Sawyers, Althy and Chris, Emmy and Debby.

"You climb up here on the seat beside me, Bonnie," said Father. "You and Mary and Miss Cora."

High on the wagon seat, Bonnie and Mary settled themselves snugly between Father and Miss Cora. Miss Cora opened her little umbrella and held it over them. The others nestled down close together in the bed of the wagon. They spread over themselves the old quilts Father had brought along. They opened all their umbrellas. Then they began to sing.

"To grandmother's house we go,
Heigh-ho! Heigh-ho!"

Down the road toward the river they went. Bonnie craned her neck to see the footbridge.

There it was, with one end broken loose, floating in the middle of the angry river.

Cautiously Father drove the horses into the muddy water below the bridge. He talked to them gently. Bonnie could scarcely hear him above the singing.

"Easy there, Mag! Go on, Joe. Easy, now. Easy. Get up, Joe. Don't be afraid!"

Deeper and deeper plunged the horses into the muddy water. They snorted and strained and pulled as Father talked to them.

"Good boy, Joe! Get up, Mag! Steady, Mag!"

Higher and higher on the horses swirled the river.

"Easy, Joe! Get up, Mag! Don't be afraid!"

"Oh-h-h! It looks like they're swimming!" cried Bonnie.

"We're almost through, Mag. Easy, now. Get up, Joe!" coaxed Father.

At last the horses pulled the wagon out of the river onto the bank. But Father didn't go straight home. He drove first to the Wattersons' house where all the Wattersons got out. Miss Cora got out too, because she was spending Thanksgiving with the Wattersons.

"Tell your father to meet me at the river Friday morning," Father told Andy. "We'll fix the footbridge."

Then Father drove to the Huffs' house and the Sawyers' house. At the Huffs', he lifted Mary out of the high seat and put her on the ground. He sent word to Mr. Huff and Mr. Sawyer to come and help him fix the footbridge Friday morning.

It was almost dark when they came in sight of their own house. The rain had stopped and the sky was clearing. The wind was turning cold. A light was shining in the kitchen.

"Oh!" cried Bonnie. "There's Mother, standing at the window!" She turned to Father. "I was a little bit scared," she said. "Just a little bit. Were you?"

Father didn't say yes or no. Instead, he said, "Tomorrow is Thanksgiving, and I know what I'm thankful for. I'm thankful everyone is safe and sound at home."

The Christmas Angel

ON MONDAY Miss Cora asked Althy and Margy Sawyer to help her assign the parts in the Christmas play.

They chose Chris for the farmer, and Ellen Watterson for the farmer's wife. They chose Andy Watterson for the lost old man who wandered to the farmer's house on Christmas Eve. They chose Jimmy Sawyer for Peter, who was to open the door for the old man, and they chose Emmy for Elsa, who was the first to see the Christmas angel coming across the starlit meadow.

They chose five other boys and girls for the children of the farmer and his wife. And they chose boys and girls for the neighbors who came to see the Christmas angel.

"Bonnie," asked Miss Cora, "how would you like to be the Christmas angel."

"I can if you want me to," said Bonnie.

"Mother will make her a white robe," said Althy.

"And I believe Mother could make her some wings," said Emmy.

That night while Bonnie dried the dishes for

105

Althy, Mother found an old sheet and made a robe for Bonnie that covered her from her chin down to her feet. Father found some chicken wire, and Emmy found some white paper, and Mother made Bonnie some wings to fasten to the back of the robe.

The next day Bonnie took the robe and the wings to school. When the lessons were finished, the boys and girls practiced the Christmas play. Althy and Margy Sawyer pulled the curtains, prompted Andy and Chris when they forgot their lines, and helped the children put on their costumes.

They were going to give the play the last afternoon of school. All their fathers and mothers would come to see it. All their grandfathers and grandmothers, and all their brothers and sisters too little for school would come to see it. Even the little babies who couldn't walk or talk would be there to see it.

Chris wore Father's worn old coat, and Father's shoes with holes in them, and he hobbled along on Grandfather Watterson's cane. Chris had many lines to say. Every night he stood in the kitchen and recited his lines to Mother while she cooked supper. Bonnie set the table for Mother and listened. Mother said she was anxious to hear Chris in the play on the last day of school.

Emmy wore a dress that Mother had worn when she was a girl. She looked as pretty as an old-fashioned picture. Every night after supper Emmy put on the dress and recited her lines while Mother sat by the fire and listened. Bonnie sat by the fire and listened too. Emmy was going to be especially good in the play, Mother said. She wouldn't miss seeing Emmy the last day of school.

Debby wasn't actually in the play. She didn't come out on the stage where people could see her. But at one point in the play where the directions said, "Music Offstage," Debby stood behind the curtain and sang an old, old Christmas carol. Every night before she went upstairs to bed, she stood in front of the fire and sang for Mother.

> "*This very night*
> *I saw a sight,*
> *A star as bright as day.*
> *And ever among*
> *A maiden song,*
>   *Lulley, by, by, lully, lulley.*"

As Bonnie pulled off her shoes by the fire, she listened too.

"That's my favorite Christmas song," said Mother. "I used to sing it when I was your age, and I'm anxious to hear you sing it in the play, Debby."

Sometimes Bonnie was sorry she was the Christmas angel, because there were no lines to say, no songs to sing for Mother.

"You can show Mother how an angel looks," said Debby.

Bonnie showed Mother how an angel looks.

"You're a very happy looking angel, Bonnie," said Mother. "I'm anxious to see you in the play."

It was then the next to the last week of school and something happened. Mother became sick. The doctor said she must stay in bed several days.

"Can't she see the Christmas play the last day of school?" Bonnie asked him.

"No, Bonnie," he said. "Your mother will be up by next Friday. But she mustn't go out of the house. Next year she may see the Christmas play. But not this year."

Mother smiled at Bonnie. "You mustn't look so sad," she said. "A Christmas angel ought to look happy."

But try as hard as she would, Bonnie could not forget that Mother could not see the Christmas play.

There were many things to do the last week of school to get ready for the play. The boys and girls made ropes of pine boughs which they gathered on the mountains, and hung over the door and the windows. The needles on the boughs were long and dark.

"Smell it!" sniffed Chris when the room was decked with green.

Margy Sawyer sniffed. "It smells cool and dark," she said.

"It smells clean and spicy, like a mountain top," sniffed Althy.

"It smells like Christmas," sniffed Emmy.

Bonnie sniffed too. "I wish Mother could smell it," she said.

Another day the boys and girls brought holly
sprays from the woods. Althy and Margy Sawyer
chose the sprays with the biggest clusters of red
berries, made a big wreath of them, and hung it
on the door.

"That must be the biggest wreath in the
world," said Andy Watterson.

"It says 'Christmas' as plainly as if it talked,"
said Emmy.

"It makes me wish we had Christmas every
day," said Debby.

"I wish Mother could see it," said Bonnie.

On Friday, as soon as the boys and girls had eaten their lunch, they swept the schoolhouse for the last time and dusted all the desks. They collected their books, their slates and tablets and pencils, and stacked them neatly out of sight in their desks to take home with them when the play was over.

They erased the blackboard, cleaned the erasers, and put the chalk away until next year. Then they put on their costumes and gathered behind the curtain.

Now and then Bonnie, wearing the long white robe and the stiff white wings Mother had made, peeped from behind the curtain to watch the people coming into the schoolhouse. Fathers and mothers, grandfathers and grandmothers were coming. Little brothers and sisters were being led along by the hand, their eyes big and full of wonder as they stared about them. And mothers carried in their arms babies too little to walk or talk.

Bonnie saw Davy Watterson's mother and Jimmy Sawyer's mother. She saw Mary Huff's mother carrying Mary's baby sister in her arms.

Miss Cora came behind the curtain to see that everyone was ready. She caught sight of Bonnie.

"Why, Bonnie!" she said. "What's the matter? You don't look like a very happy angel. Even your wings look droopy."

"I was wishing . . ." began Bonnie.

"Wishing what?" asked Miss Cora.

"Do you suppose . . ."

"What is it, Bonnie?" asked Miss Cora.

"Do you suppose . . ."

Miss Cora smiled at her. "I believe you must be thinking of something special now, Bonnie," she said. "You are looking happy once more, as a Christmas angel ought to look."

Bonnie stood on tiptoe and whispered something in Miss Cora's ear.

"Why, Bonnie!" said Miss Cora. "Maybe we could."

She stood a moment, thinking.

"I believe we can do that, Bonnie," she said. She thought about it another minute.

"No, there's no reason why we can't do it," she said. "And we will do it. You leave everything to me."

Everybody said Bonnie was the happiest Christmas angel that had ever been seen in the schoolhouse in the woods. But Bonnie, when the play was over, hurried to find Father. She put her knapsack across her shoulder. In it were her first reader, her slate, broken now, and only a little piece of her slate pencil.

"I'm ready to go home, Father," she said.

"What's your hurry?" Father asked.

"It's a secret," she said. "It's a Christmas surprise."

At home, everyone talked at once, telling Mother about the Christmas play. They all talked, that is, all but Bonnie. She said no more than she had said in the play. But she looked very wise.

She hurried through her chores. She heaped the stovewood box high. She set the table for Althy, who was getting supper for Mother, and she dried the dishes for Emmy, three plates at a time.

When the dishes were finished, they gathered around the fire, Mother sitting in her special rocking chair. They were still talking about the Christmas play.

"Listen!" said Chris. "I hear something!"

"I do too," said Althy.

They grew quiet and listened.

"Sounds like a wagon," said Emmy.

"Somebody's coming," said Debby.

The noise stopped at the front gate.

"I believe it's somebody coming here," said Mother.

"Somebody is coming here!" cried Bonnie, jumping up from the floor where she was sitting. "Everybody is coming. And we're going to give the Christmas play for Mother right in this room."

She ran to the door. When she flung it open, all the boys and girls from school, all their fathers and mothers, their grandfathers and grandmothers, the brothers and sisters too little to go to school, and the little babies who were already sound asleep were outside. With them was Miss Cora, carrying the big holly wreath.

"Merry Christmas!" they called to Mother. And Miss Cora hung the holly wreath over the fireplace especially for Mother.

There was never such a hustle and bustle as they made ready to give the play for Mother. For a curtain Chris and Andy, with Father's help, stretched two blankets across a corner of the room, so that Althy and Margy Sawyer could pull them. Father and Mr. Watterson moved Mother's chair to the center of the room so that she could see everything, since the play was especially for her.

In the kitchen the boys and girls put on their

costumes. When Althy pinned Bonnie's wings on her back, Bonnie opened the door a crack and peeped at Mother. This was the very best school day of all, she thought.

She was still thinking it was the best day of school when it was time for her to go on the stage, and she went walking across the kitchen which was a starlit meadow, and out in front of the people.

And when the play was over, and Althy sat down at the organ to play Christmas carols, she was sure there had never been a happier day in all

her life. Everyone sang. They stood about the
organ, all but Mother, who sat in her chair by
the fire and listened. They sang *Down in Yon
Forest* and *Jesus Born in Bethany*. They sang

Sing, All Men. And when they had finished *As I Sat Under a Sycamore Tree,* they played a game of forfeits as they sang *The Twelve Days of Christmas.*

> "The twelfth day of Christmas
>   My true love sent to me
>   Twelve lords a-leaping,
>   Eleven ladies dancing,
>   Ten pipers piping,
>   Nine drummers drumming,
>   Eight maids a-milking,
>   Seven swans a-swimming,
>   Six geese a-laying,
>   Five golden rings,
>   Four colley birds,
>   Three French hens,
>   Two turtle doves, and
>   A partridge in a pear-tree."

Last of all, Debby stood close to the organ and sang, sweet and clear,

"A lovely lady sat and sang
And to her Son thus 'gan to say:
My Son, My Lord, my dear darling,
Why liest Thou thus in hay?
My own dear Son,
How art thou come?
Art thou not God verily?
But nevertheless
I will not cease
To sing: 'By, by, lully, lulley.'"

And everyone sang with her,

"This very night
I saw a sight,
A star as bright as any day,
And ever among
A maiden song,
Lulley, by, by, lully, lulley."

Then it was time to go home. Mother thanked them for coming. It was a Christmas she would never forget, she said.

"Good-bye, and Merry Christmas!" called everybody.

"Good-bye till next year!" the boys and girls called to Miss Cora.

"Good-bye until next August!" said Miss Cora.

Finally the door was shut and the sound of the wagons died away down the frozen road. Father turned to Bonnie. "What's wrong with the Christmas angel now?" he asked. "Why is she so sad all of a sudden?"

"Because this is the last day of school," said Bonnie.

They started to bed then. When Bonnie was ready for bed, she found Debby's books. "This book belongs to Debby," she read on the flyleaf of each book.

With Debby's pencil, Bonnie erased "Debby" on every flyleaf, and wrote "Bonnie." "This book belongs to Bonnie," the flyleaves read now.

Upstairs Bonnie stacked the books neatly on the end of the bench.

"What are you doing that for?" asked Debby.

"I'm getting ready for school next August," said Bonnie.